Dear Mr. Leprechaun
LETTERS FROM MY FIRST FRIENDSHIP

To Scholastic Book Club:

Wishing you good luck and true friendship forever!

May 2004

Albert Nelson Burton

by MARTIN NELSON BURTON

illustrated by CLINT HANSEN

LONDON TOWN PRESS

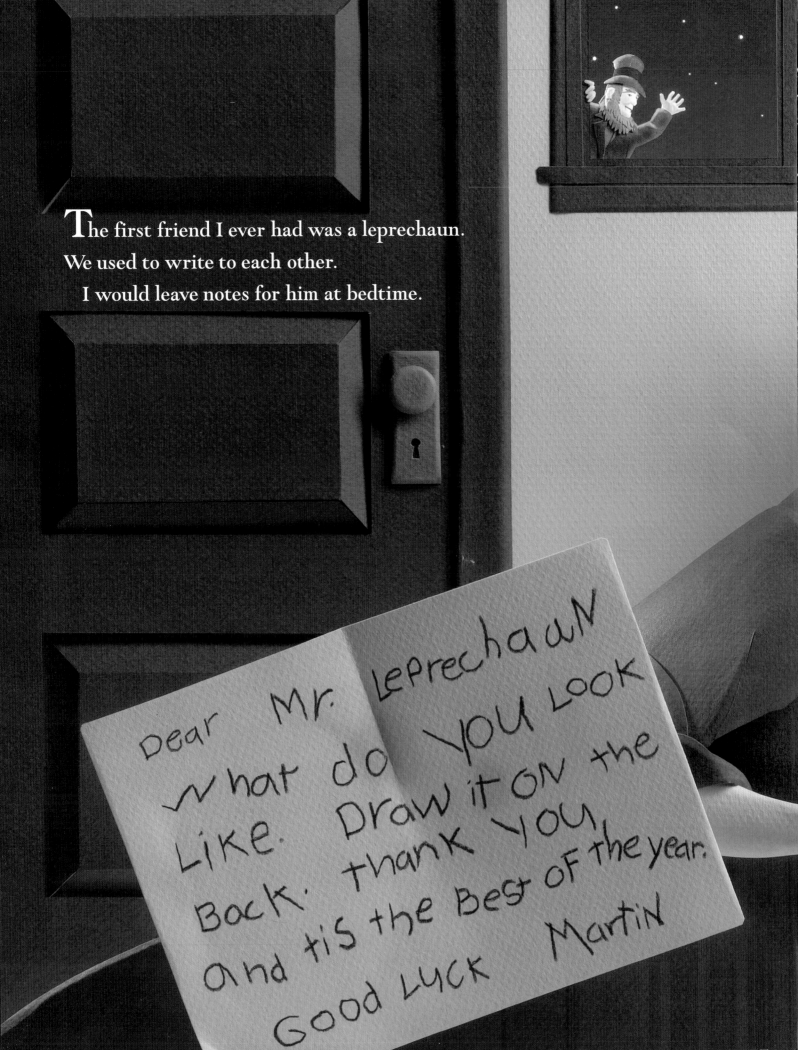

The first friend I ever had was a leprechaun.
We used to write to each other.
I would leave notes for him at bedtime.

Dear Mr. Leprechaun
What do you look
Like. Draw it on the
Back. Thank you,
and tis the Best of the year.
Good Luck Martin

He would write back to me while I slept.
In the morning, I would find his answer.

Like most leprechauns,
mine was full of mischief.

DEAR MARTIN:
IT HAS BEEN A BUSY LIFE FOR ME, AS
YOU KNOW I TRAVEL AROUND ALOT, JUMPING
HERE AND THERE, TRICKING PEOPLE AND
TRYING NOT TO GET CAUGHT, AND PROTECTING
MY POT OF GOLD.

But he was nice to me.
Sometimes he would fix my broken toys,
or untangle the strings of my marionette.

Whenever I asked for some real leprechaun magic,
though, he would always find some reason
not to do it.

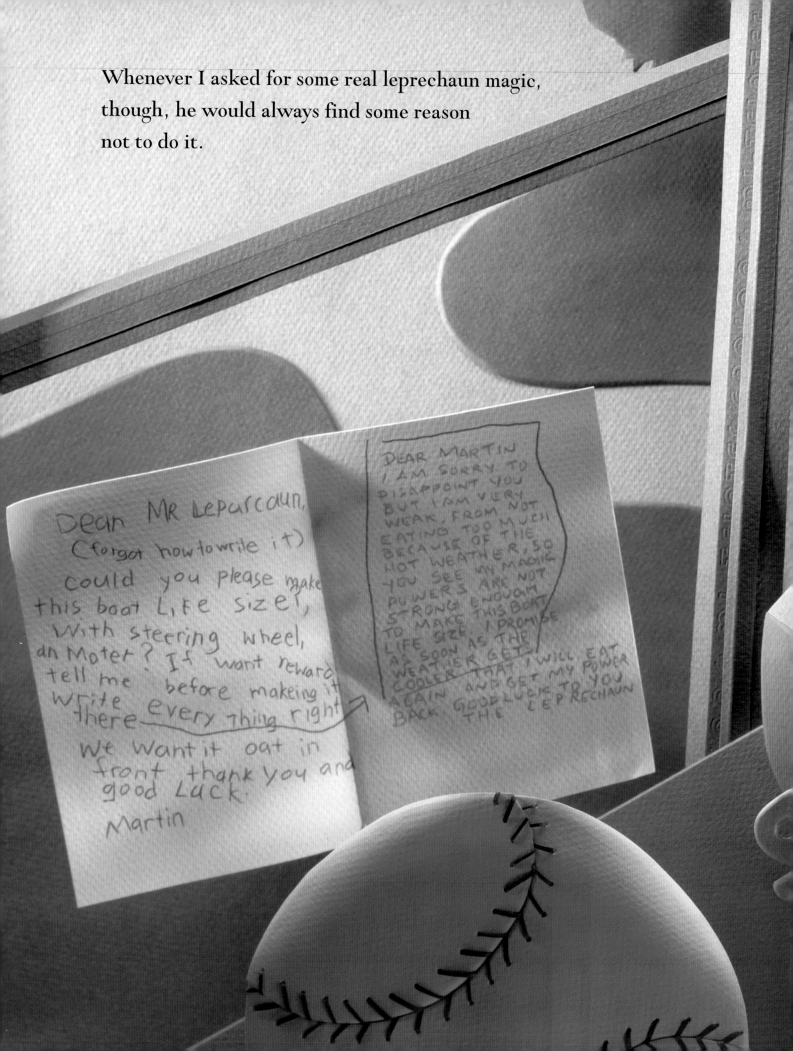

Dear Mr Leparcaun,
(forgot how to write it)

could you please make
this boat Life size',
with steering wheel,
an Moter? If want reward
tell me before makeing it
write there every thing right

We want it oat in
front thank you and
good Luck.
Martin

DEAR MARTIN
I AM SORRY TO
DISAPPOINT YOU
BUT I AM VERY
WEAK, FROM NOT
EATING TOO MUCH
BECAUSE OF THE
HOT WEATHER, SO
YOU SEE MY MAGIC
POWERS ARE NOT
STRONG ENOUGH
TO MAKE THIS BOAT
LIFE SIZE, I PROMISE
AS SOON AS THE
WEATHER GETS
COOLER THAT I WILL EAT
AGAIN AND GET MY POWER
BACK. GOODLUCK TO YOU
THE LEPRECHAUN

I was also nice to him. If Mr. Leprechaun told me he was not feeling well, I would make him his favorite treat: dandelion tea.

Dear MR. Leperchaun
This is for you TO
Drink will you please try
your best to get well.
it makes me sad to see
you without your powers.
Do+ Not write a note Back.
Martin.

Mr. Leprechaun loved to boast about how he could snap his fingers, disappear from wherever he was, and suddenly reappear wherever he wanted to be.

I could never get him to tell me how he did this, though I asked him over and over.

MARTIN YOU ARE TRYING TO TRICK ME AGAIN! YOU WANT ME TO TELL YOU MY SECRET ABOUT HOW I MAKE MYSELF VANISH. I CAN NOT DO THAT, FOR YOU WOULD PROBABLY HOLD MY FINGERS SO I COULD NOT SNAP THEM.

Mr. Leprechaun could sometimes be such a frustrating little fellow.

More than anything, I wanted to see him for myself.
During the summer, my dad and I began to sit outside
in the evenings and look for leprechauns in the trees.

My mom brought home books about the "little people"
and read me stories from Ireland about their pranks.

But, unlike the leprechauns I would read about, mine never
showed himself. He'd tell me that he couldn't play on my baseball
team because he had to go back to Ireland to pick potatoes.

Or that he couldn't take me to Leprechaun Land because I
might steal his pot of gold.

Or that he couldn't make me a tree
house because he had to get ready for
a big St. Patrick's Day party.

Finally, I told him I'd be
happy with just a photograph
of himself and a trip to Ireland.

Still, I kept on writing to him.
Even after I learned cursive.

Dear MR. L.

How DO YOU LIKE our Bedroom? I think it is great! My father is going to buy shelves for our bedroom. Don't you wish you were as lucky as us? By the way, are you a man? OK By the other way, Did you find my Grandpa and see me a way to get to Ireland? (next summer, of course). I still love you very much. I'll try to do my best in everything but I need a little luck from you.

Yes great!

Bye, (Martin Burton)

DEAR MARTIN
YES I LIKE YOUR BED ROOM VERY MUCH, YOU & YOUR BROTHER (WHAT IS HIS NAME) ARE VERY LUCKEY YES I AM A MAN, NOT A VERY LARGE MAN, BUT A MAN NEVER THE LESS. YES I HAVE JUST ABOUT MADE ALL THE ARRANGEMENTS FOR YOU & YOUR GRANDPA TO COME OVER TO IRELAND ONE OF THESE SUMMERS (SOON) I LOVE YOU & YOUR FAMILY VERY MUCH, TOO, MARTIN I WILL GIVE YOU ALL THE LUCK YOU NEED, FOR EVER & EVER.
LOVE YOU ALWAYS, MR. L

Dear Mr.
Ho

At times, however, he would beg me not to leave any more messages.

I WILL SHOW MYSELF VERY
VERY SOON, BUT DON'T HOLD YOUR
BREATH.
I DO NOT LIKE YOU TO WRITE
NOTES WHEN I AM SO BUSY. BECAUSE
IT TAKES TOO MUCH TIME TO ANSWER.
THIS PENCIL IS SO BIG AND I AM SO
LITTLE THAT, IT WEARS ME OUT.
WRITE ME ABOUT 2 WEEKS
AFTER ST. PATS DAY. THAT SHOW
ME TIME TO REST SHOW
YOU TOO

Even my own father, for some reason,
became weary of all my letter writing...

MR. L.
My father said: "Don't write a
note tonight. I don't have time to
bother with you." I was wandering
what that meant? Well, anyway
I wanted to do something to you
What could I do? I want to help
you could I? And if I could, what
could I do ? Sincerly Yours, Marty
Dear Marty,
Your father loves you very
much, he did not mean that
he "Don't have time for you." he
means that he does not have time
to help me (Mr. L) Well there is
nothing that I need right now
but I will write later and
tell you. Bye Mr. L.

Dear MR. Leperchaun

First Car

As I grew older, slowly I began to write to him less and less often. Over the years, as happens from time to time even to the best of friends, I gradually lost touch with Mr. Leprechaun.

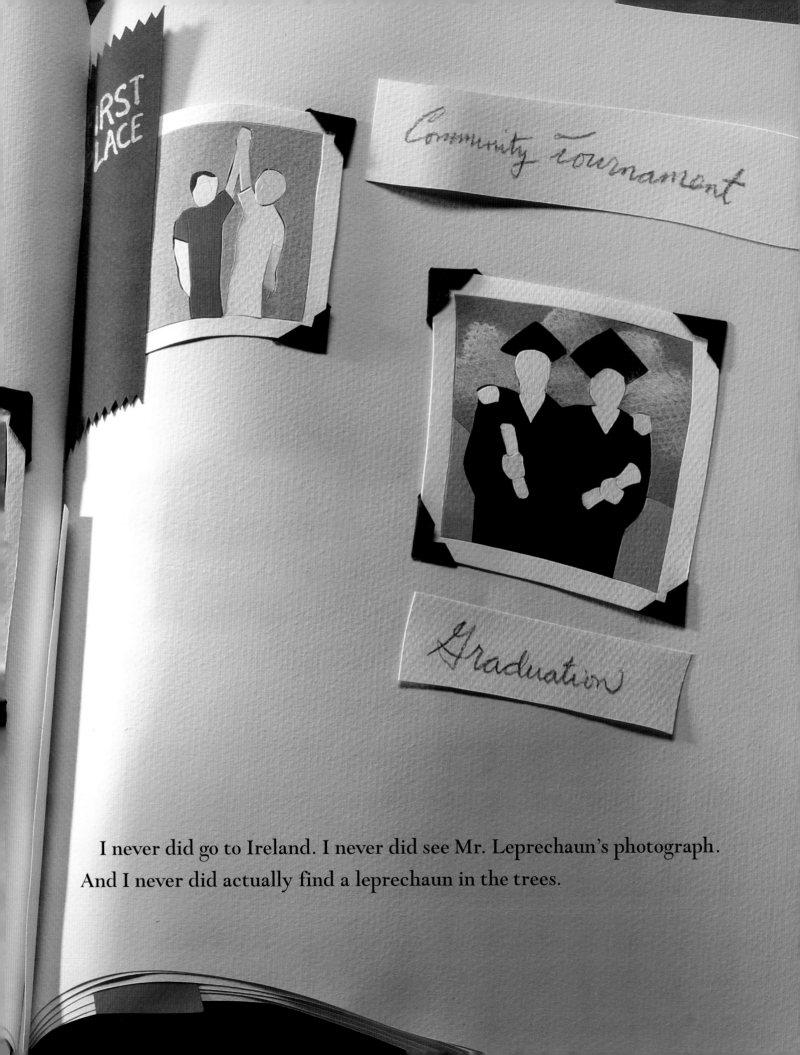

I never did go to Ireland. I never did see Mr. Leprechaun's photograph.
And I never did actually find a leprechaun in the trees.

But one thing I will always remember. No matter how busy, or tired, or weak he may have been, how heavy the pencil, or how impossible my requests, still he managed to reply to every single note I ever wrote.

Though I stopped writing him long ago, somehow I feel he never left me. Even now, I am sure he is somewhere close by. Wherever he is, I love him still with all my heart.

And if I ever do catch that leprechaun, I'm going to grab
his fingers and hold them tight so he cannot snap them. Then
we'll sit down together, sip on dandelion tea, and talk about
the good old days until the sun comes up in the morning.

A TRUE STORY

If my father had not carefully rescued each note that Mr. Leprechaun and I so casually exchanged, from my first writing at age five through our last letters after I turned eleven, our remarkable correspondence would surely have been lost for all time. Instead, the entire collection came to rest safely within his bedroom dresser drawer. When he finally decided to return the notes to me, I was three decades older.

In these pages, Clint Hansen has re-created each original message by hand, making only small cosmetic changes as absolutely necessary. Thus restored, the notes appear exactly as Mr. Leprechaun and I wrote them to each other so many years ago.

Martin Nelson Burton
La Cañada Flintridge, California
March, 2003

For Mr. Leprechaun
—MNB

For Jacob, Rachel and Rebekah
—CH

Photographer Dean Tanner stages Clint Hansen's artwork.

The illustrations were created in paper sculpture. In this medium, construction paper is cut,
shaped, and then glued together in multiple layers to form three-dimensional figures. Each piece
is then positioned on an illuminated studio set, and the finished scene is photographed.

The notes were replicated with colored pencil on construction paper.

Photography by Dean Tanner of Primary Image, Des Moines, Iowa.

Text copyright © 2003 by Martin Nelson Burton.
Illustrations copyright © 2003 by Clint Hansen.
All rights reserved. This book, or parts thereof, may not be reproduced
in any form without permission in writing from the publisher.

London Town Press P.O. Box 585 Montrose, California 91021-0585.
www.LondonTownPress.com

Printed in Hong Kong by South China Printing Co. (1988) Ltd.
Book design by Christy Hale.
10 9 8 7 6 5 4 3 2

Publisher's Cataloging-in-Publication Data
Burton, Martin Nelson.
Dear Mr. Leprechaun : letters from my first friendship / by Martin Nelson Burton ;
illustrated by Clint Hansen. —1st ed.
p. cm.
SUMMARY: The author reflects on his childhood correspondence with a leprechaun who—in the
handwriting style of the child's father—taught him the true meaning of steadfast friendship.
Audience: Ages 4—9.
LCCN 2002094901
ISBN 0-9666490-0-1
1. Friendship—Juvenile literature. 2. Leprechauns—Juvenile literature. 3. Burton, Martin Nelson—Correspondence—Juvenile literature.
[1. Friendship. 2. Leprechauns. 3. Burton, Martin Nelson—Correspondence.]
I. Hansen, Clint. II. Title
BJ1533.F8B87 2003   177'.62